Disney's My Very First Winnie the Pooh™

Pooh's Fun with One

Written by
Cynthia Michaels

Illustrated by
Fernando Guell, Paul Lopez,
Angel Rodrigues, Eva Rodrigues

SCHOLASTIC INC.

New York Toronto London Auckland Sydney
Mexico City New Delhi Hong Kong Buenos Aires

Published by Scholastic Inc., 90 Old Sherman Turnpike, Danbury, CT 06816
by arrangement with Disney Licensed Publishing.

SCHOLASTIC and associated logos are trademarks
and/or registered trademarks of Scholastic Inc.

ISBN 0-7172-8921-4

Printed in the U.S.A.

It was morning in the Hundred-Acre Wood.
Birds were singing in the trees and meadows. But
Pooh was still sound asleep, happily dreaming
that birds were playing around his room.

Suddenly, there in his dream was Piglet, flying
with the birds!

"Pooh," whistled Piglet. "Do you want to
play with us?"

"Yes, I do," said Pooh in
his dream.

Then Pooh woke up. He
looked around, but nobody
was there.

"Oh," he sighed. "It was only a dream. But,
I still want to play."

Suddenly, a pretty bluebird flew onto Pooh's windowsill and chirped.

"Oh, good morning, little bird," Pooh said cheerfully. "Would you like to play with me?" But the bluebird flew away. As Pooh was watching him go, Owl flew by.

"Hello, Owl!" called Pooh. "Would you like to play with me?"

"I'm afraid I simply haven't the time at present, Pooh," Owl answered. "But perhaps tomorrow you could come to tea?"

"Yes, all right," Pooh called as Owl flew out of sight. "Good-bye, Owl," he added softly.

"Oh, well," said Pooh, "I shall have breakfast."

As the sun rose higher and higher in the sky, the honey got lower and lower in the pot. Soon Pooh was licking up the last drop of honey.

"Mmm. Too bad Owl was busy," said Pooh, smacking his lips. "This was a yummy breakfast he missed."

"Now," said Pooh as he went out into the Hundred-Acre Wood, "I think I'll go find Piglet. Maybe he can play with me today."

But Piglet wasn't at home.

"Perhaps Rabbit is not busy yet," thought Pooh, continuing on to Rabbit's house.

"I can't play today, Pooh," Rabbit called from his garden. "I've got to wash my clothes and weed my garden and . . . and . . . water my flowers and . . . sweep my floor."

"Maybe tomorrow morning, then?" Pooh said, waving good-bye. "Oh, well," he sighed. "I shall find someone else to play with me."

But it seemed that *everyone* in the Hundred-Acre Wood was busy that morning.

Kanga was busy giving Roo a bath.

Gopher was busy digging a new tunnel.

Even Eeyore was busy gathering thistles.
"They're ripe," Eeyore told Pooh. "Have to
pick 'em now. Nobody else will."

Pooh sat down under a tree. He sat there, wondering who else could play with him, when along came Piglet.

"Hello, Piglet!" Pooh waved to his friend.

"Hello, Pooh," said Piglet. "I'm on my way to Rabbit's house. I promised to help him today."

"Oh. Then I expect you're also too busy to play," Pooh said sadly.

"But we can play tomorrow," Piglet promised, waving good-bye.

"Maybe Christopher Robin will play with me," sighed Pooh, and he set off to find out.

"Oh, I'd like to play with you, Pooh," said Christopher Robin, "but I'm going to my grandmother's today."

Then, because Pooh looked so sad, Christopher Robin added, "I do have time for a little walk, if you'd like."

"Yes, I would," said Pooh, cheering up a bit. So the two friends walked hand-in-hand. Suddenly, Christopher Robin cried, "Look! There's Tigger!"

Tigger was bouncing. "Helloo, Pooh! Helloo, Christopher Robin!" Tigger called. "Can't stop! I'm so-o-o busy bouncin'!"

He bounced right over a fence, and away he went.

Pooh and Christopher Robin sat down together.

"Christopher Robin? I'm not a very busy bear today," Pooh confessed sadly. "But everyone else is busy. There's no one to play with me."

"I understand, Pooh," said Christopher Robin. "It's always fun to play with a friend. But sometimes it can be fun to play on your own."

"All alone?" questioned Pooh.

Christopher Robin nodded. "Just think of fun things you like to do, and then do them by yourself."

Pooh thought it over. "I'll try," he said.

Christopher Robin hugged his friend, but then he had to say good-bye.

Pooh sat in the sun and tried to think of something fun to do. But his rumbly tummy was making so much noise, he couldn't hear himself think.

"Perhaps I should have a smackerel for lunch. Then I'll be able to think properly."

So Pooh got a pot of honey from home and had a picnic outside all by himself. It turned out to be a very fun thing to do!

After lunch, Pooh played on the swing.

Up . . . up . . . UP! went Pooh.

Back . . . back . . . BACK! went Pooh. It felt like flying, just like Piglet in his dream!

"What a fun thing to do by myself," Pooh thought. Now he was excited to find more things to do alone. He ran inside for the blue balloon Christopher Robin had given him yesterday. "Balloons like to fly, too!"

The wind was strong. Pooh was having such a lovely time flying with the balloon that he didn't notice the darkening clouds until a raindrop plopped on his nose.

Just then, Kanga came hopping by with Roo.

"Hurry inside, Pooh, dear," called Kanga. "Don't catch cold."

"Isn't the rain great!" cried Roo. "April showers bring May flowers!" he called back to Pooh as Kanga hopped away.

Pooh hurried home, but the rain hadn't brought him any flowers at all. Then the bear of very little brain had a very big idea. He would make some flowers all by himself!

Pooh found paper, crayons, and glue, and soon he made himself a beautiful flower!

When he was done, Pooh made a game of cleaning up his paper and glue.

"Hmm," he thought. "A little rumbly is telling me it's dinnertime. I believe that I shall have my favorite bee-tree honey for dinner."

As the sun began to dip low in the sky, Pooh began to dip his paw into the honey pot.

Eating honey indoors was fun, too!

After dinner, Pooh was extra sticky, so he decided to take a bath. Pooh played happily in the bubbles. He even sang a little song:

When you're playing in the tub,
You wash and clean and scrub and scrub,
Making bubbles, sailing boats,
Splashing with a duck that floats.
Bath time is a lot of fun!
Plus, you'll be clean when
you are done!

Bath time *was* lots of fun!

Pooh felt all clean and warm after his bath
but he wasn't very sleepy yet.

"I know what!" exclaimed Pooh. "Perhaps
I might tell myself a bedtime story . . . or two."
He snuggled into his cozy chair to look at
some books.

Pooh couldn't read the words, but it was
fun to look at the pictures and make up his
own stories to go with them.

"Christopher Robin was right,"
Pooh thought. "I had a very fun
day doing things all by myself!"
But he did look forward to
tomorrow, when his friends
would have time to play again.

Soon, Pooh's eyes felt heavy, so he climbed into bed. He began to count sheep, but he drifted right off to sleep. So the sheep counted him!

One tired Pooh bear had a lot of fun,
Playing games by himself 'til the day
was done.